How MANY SLEEPS 'TIL CHRISTMAS?

Published in 2021 by Mortimer Children's Books
An Imprint of Welbeck Children's Limited,
part of Welbeck Publishing Group.
20 Mortimer Street London W1T 3JW

Text & Illustrations © Welbeck Children's Limited,
part of Welbeck Publishing Group.

Designer: Deborah Vickers
Editor: Jenni Lazell

A CIP catalogue record for this book is available from
the British Library

978-1-83935-087-0

Printed in Heshan, China
10 9 8 7 6 5 4 3 2 1

HOW MANY SLEEPS 'TIL CHRISTMAS?

JOFF BROWN

MORTIMER

GABRIELE TAFUNI

The weather is colder – December is here.
There's a fabulous feeling of seasonal cheer.
And old folk and young are beginning to say...

HOW MANY SLEEPS 'TIL
CHRISTMAS DAY!

What a sweet noise from the choir outside!
It's a song about snow and a magic sleigh ride.
It's warming your heart and it's making you sway.

JUST **10** MORE SLEEPS 'TIL
CHRISTMAS DAY!

When buying your presents, don't think of amounts.
It's not the cost – it's the thought that counts.
It's going to be fun when you give them away.

JUST **9** MORE SLEEPS 'TIL CHRISTMAS DAY!

The first winter snowflake falls in the night.
By the morning, the world's in a blanket of white.
Will it keep on snowing? How long will it stay?

JUST **8** MORE SLEEPS 'TIL
CHRISTMAS DAY!

Let's make paper chains, like they did long ago
to give every home a holiday glow.
Add a wreath for our door, or a mistletoe spray.

JUST **7** MORE SLEEPS 'TIL
CHRISTMAS DAY!

Put twinkling lights on your Christmas tree
and a fairy might land there, just wait and see.
If you're very lucky, she might choose to stay.

JUST **6** MORE SLEEPS 'TIL CHRISTMAS DAY!

While kids are asleep, all the snowmen get moving.
They hold 'snow-balls' full of feasting and grooving.
They're dancing the tango, the floss and ballet.

JUST **5** MORE SLEEPS 'TIL CHRISTMAS DAY!

Let's build a house made of gingerbread dough,
with gumdrops for doorknobs, and icing for snow.
Don't eat it yet! It's a lovely display.

JUST **4** MORE SLEEPS 'TIL
CHRISTMAS DAY!

Santa's reindeer are practicing all their best moves.
They swoop through the sky on their magical hooves.
They can't wait to pull Santa's wonderful sleigh.

JUST **3** MORE SLEEPS 'TIL CHRISTMAS DAY!

In Santa's factory, all the elves he employs
are racing like crazy to finish the toys.
"Keep going!" calls Santa. "There's no time for play!"

JUST **2** MORE SLEEPS 'TIL CHRISTMAS DAY!

The night before Christmas, when everyone's sleeping,
Santa visits each house – so remember, no peeping!
But if you listen closely, you might hear him say...

JUST **1** MORE SLEEP 'TIL
CHRISTMAS DAY!

Christmas Day's here! It's the time when we share joy with our family, and show friends we care. To loved ones nearby, and to those far away...

We wish you a
WONDERFUL

CHRISTMAS DAY!

Make Christmas cookies

Make these festive treats for your family and friends to enjoy at Christmas.

You will need

- ★ 100g unsalted butter
- ★ 100g caster sugar
- ★ 275g plain flour
- ★ 1 egg
- ★ 1 tsp vanilla extract
- ★ 400g icing sugar
- ★ food colouring
- ★ edible glitter or sprinkles

- ★ baking tray
- ★ parchment paper
- ★ mixing bowl
- ★ spatula or wooden spoon
- ★ rolling pin
- ★ cookie cutters
- ★ oven (preheated to 190°C)

1 Mix the butter and caster sugar together in a bowl with a spatula until pale and creamy. Beat in the egg and vanilla extract. Then stir in the flour until the mixture becomes a dough.

2 Lightly scatter some flour onto a clean surface and use a rolling pin to roll out the dough. Try and make the dough one centimetre thick.

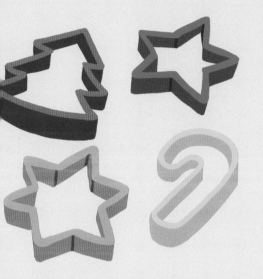

3 Line a baking tray with parchment paper. Use cookie cutters to cut shapes out of the dough, and place them onto the baking tray. Bake them in the oven for 8–10 minutes, before taking them out and leaving to cool.

4 Sift icing sugar into a mixing bowl and stir in enough water (3-4 tablespoons) to make a smooth mixture. Stir in the food colouring. Spread the icing onto the cookies with a small spatula and add any extra edible decorations.

Use a piping bag to make patterns with icing sugar!

Craft festive paper decorations

Create beautiful snowflakes to add
Christmas magic to your home.

You will need

★ plain white paper

★ safety scissors

★ tape

1 First you need to make your A4 sheet of paper
into a square. Fold down one corner to meet
the opposite edge, forming a triange. Cut
away the paper below the triangle. Now open
up the paper to show a square.

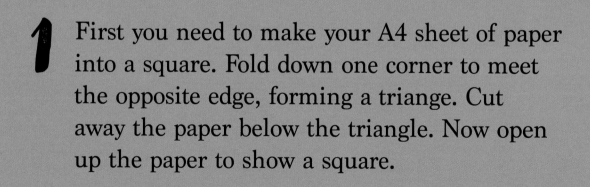

2 Fold the sheet of paper in half diagonally to make a triangle. Then fold the triange in half to make a smaller triangle.

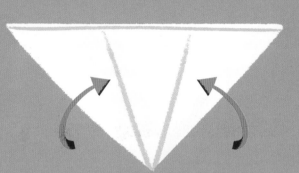

3 Splitting the triangle into three equal sections, fold the left side towards the front, then fold the right side towards the front.

4 Cut across the paper to create a straight-edged triangle.

5 Now it's time to make your snowflake shapes! Carefully snip into your wedge of paper to create a pattern.

6 Finally, open up the paper to reveal a perfect wintry snowflake!